A Leaf, a Stick, and a Stone

Written by
Maggie Felsch

Illustrated by
Larissa Sharina

© 2020 Jenny Phillips
goodandbeautiful.com

Challenge Words

sail

sword

castle

I walked to the end of the driveway today
hoping to find something new.
I wanted to see what the world had in store
for a bored little child to do.

This morning I had gone to Mama and asked,
"Can we do any fun stuff today?"

Mama kept stitching the hole in my jeans and said what she always did say.

"I have work to be done before I can play.
You go find something to do,
but if you are bored or want me to choose,
there is plenty of work for you, too."

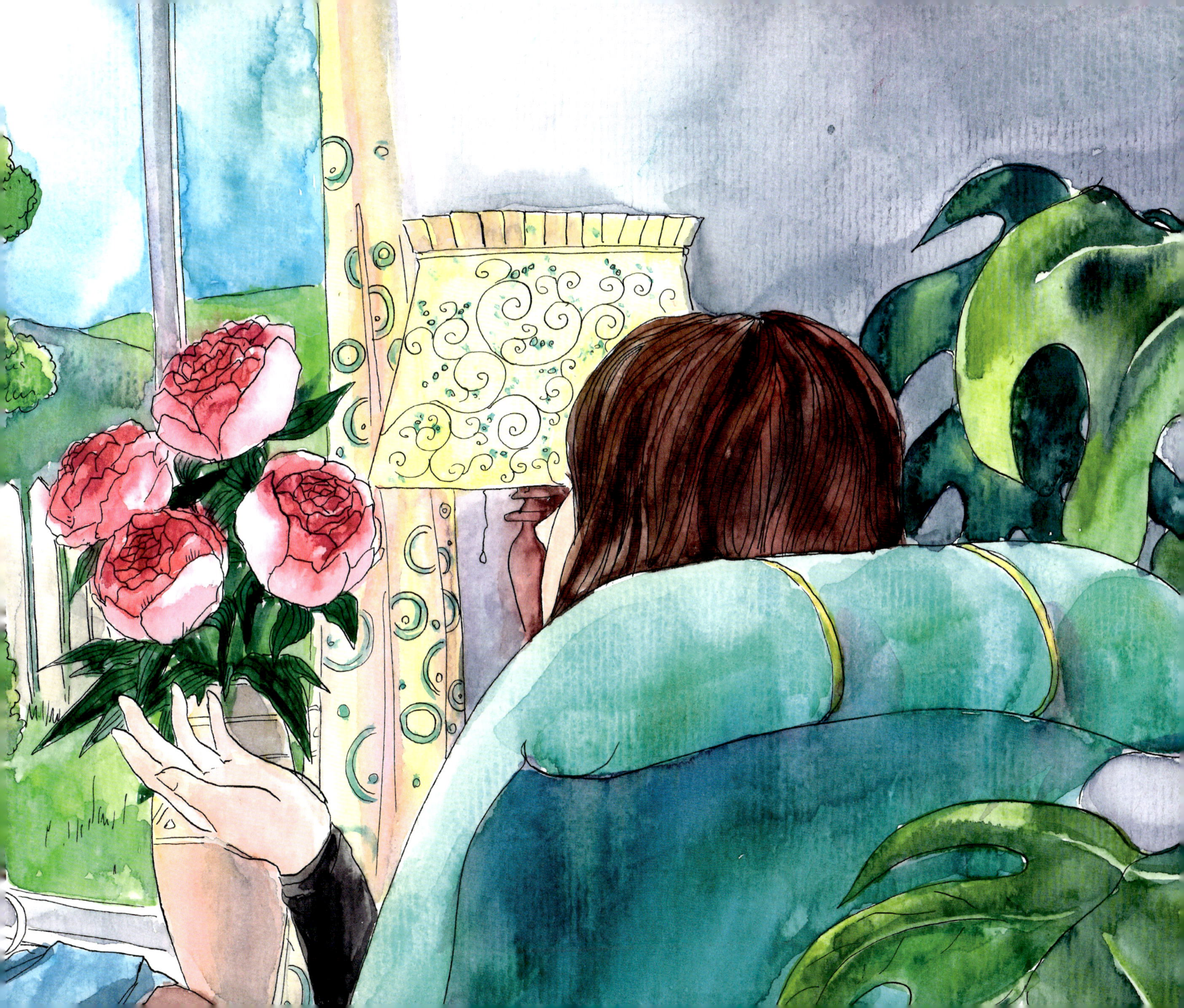

"No thanks," I had said as I left to find Dad,
hoping so much he was free.
"Dad, I am bored, and I want to have fun.
Will you go do something with me?"

Why Dad was under the front of the truck
I surely did not understand,
but he poked out his head, all covered in goo,
and patted my leg with his hand.

"The truck needs some work, so I cannot go now,
but maybe this afternoon.
Let me finish my work, and then later on
we can go fishing at the lagoon."

Fishing with Dad was going to be fun,
but I needed something fun now.
Mama had said to find something to do.
I wanted to have fun, but how?

And that is how I ended up here
at the end of the driveway alone,
looking for something, but nothing was here—

just a leaf,

a stick,

and a stone.

I hoped and waited to find something fun.
Then I felt a cool, gentle breeze.
The leaf on the ground started to shake,
and so did the leaves on the trees.

A sail! That's what the leaf looked like to me—
a sail on a ship at sea.

Then the breeze picked up, and the leaf took off, flying away so free.

I followed the ship as it sailed away,
across the sea of green.
(Yes, the sea is blue most of the time,
but this sea had grass in between.)

I saw clear as day a pirate ship
with gold and silk inside!
Pirates were sitting a-top the deck
while the breeze kept the ship a-glide.

Then a new idea for the tiny leaf ship—
the Mayflower was its name!
The little leaf ship sailing the sea
held pilgrims playing a game.

The ship soon flew from my grassy yard,
so I followed it no more,
but that was okay, for I saw a stick,
a little weapon of war.

I picked up the stick; it became my sword,
and I was a viking so brave.

I battled to save my family and land,
and I made other vikings behave.

My stick then turned into a brass baton—
I was leading a band!
The birds in the trees played the flutes and the drums,
with French horns and trumpets so grand!

Lovely music and chirps and tweets filled the sunny spring air.
The birds and I played pretty songs without a bit of care.

As the song went on, I saw something new—
a movement by my foot.
There on the stone, a wee tiny ant,
busy and black as soot.

The ant was keeping his castle safe.
His princess was inside.
The red ants on the dirt below
were the bad guys trying to hide.

Then the brave little ant crawled away from his stone.
My turn to use it, but how?
The smooth gray stone was the perfect thing
for a game of hopscotch now.

I tossed the stone. Then I began,
one foot, two feet, one.
I did not hear my dad come near,
I was having so much fun.

"Ready to catch some fish?" Dad asked.
I turned my head and looked.
"I did not even hear you come.
This hopscotch has me hooked!"

Dad smiled and said, "The truck is done.
Mama is ready, too."
How time had flown! I had such fun
and so many things to do!

And that is how my day was filled.
I no longer felt alone.
I had pirates, pilgrims, vikings, birds,

a leaf, a stick, and a stone.

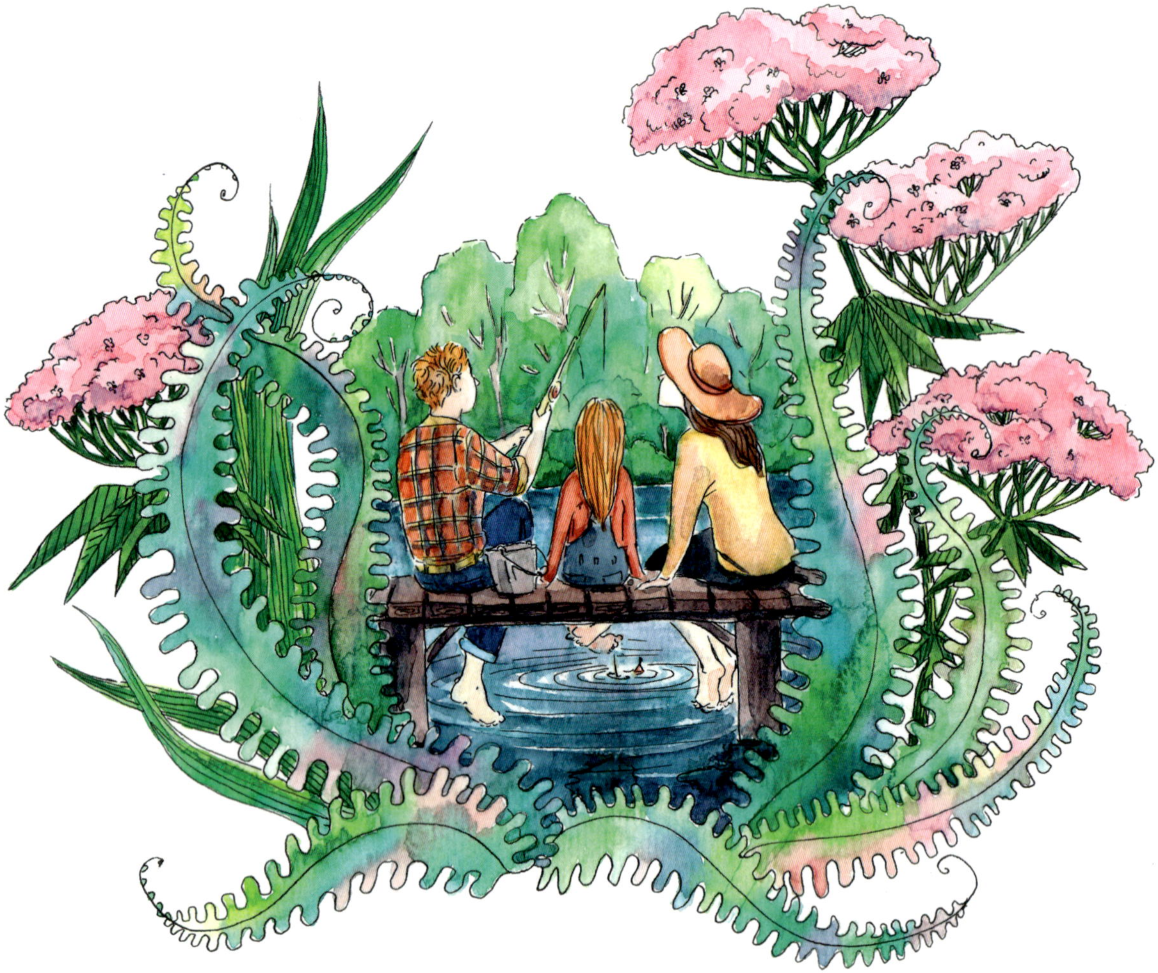